Red, White, and Blue

Written by Larry, Paris and Langston

Illustrated by Nicole Lamarr

forWord
BOOKS

John 1:1 In the beginning was the Word...

John 1:1 In the beginning was the Word...

RED WHITE AND BLUE
Published by ForWord Books
21143 Hawthorne Blvd, Ste 184
Torrance, CA 90503

Library of Congress Cataloging-in-Publication Data is available.

ISBN 979-8-9882642-6-2

Our books may be purchased in bulk for promotional, educational, or business use. Contact us via email at: ForWordBooks@gmail.com

Published in the United States by ForWord Books

**RED IS THE COLOR OF
A DELICIOUS APPLE**

**RED IS THE COLOR OF
A RAINDEER'S NOSE**

RED IS THE COLOR OF A DODGE BALL

RED IS THE COLOR OF A ROSE

RED IS THE COLOR OF A LADYBUG

RED IS THE COLOR OF A FIRE TRUCK

RED IS THE COLOR OF A CARDINAL BIRD

**RED IS THE COLOR OF
A LITTLE RED BIKE**

WHITE IS THE COLOR OF
A BUNNY RABBIT

WHITE IS THE COLOR OF
A POLAR BEAR

WHITE IS THE COLOR OF
TINY THE DOG

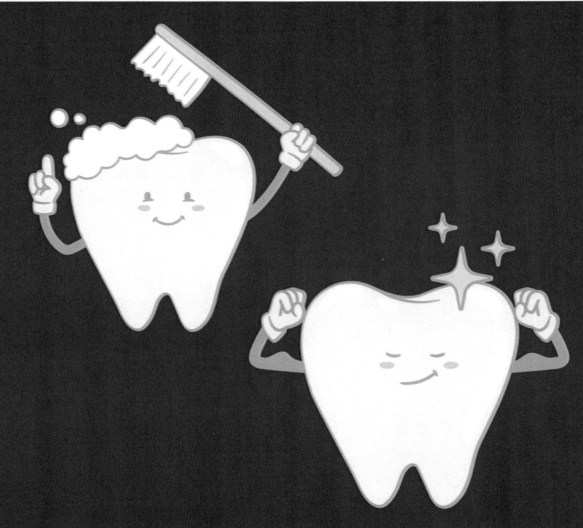

WHITE IS THE COLOR OF SHINY TEETH

WHITE IS THE COLOR OF
THE CLOUDS IN THE SKY

WHITE IS THE COLOR OF A SNOWMAN

WHITE IS THE COLOR OF A SHEEP

WHITE IS THE COLOR OF A DUCK
THAT GOES QUACK, QUACK, QUACK

**MY NAME IS CALEB
AND I LOVE THE COLOR BLUE**

BLUE IS THE COLOR OF A DOLPHIN

BLUE IS THE COLOR OF BERRIES

BLUE IS MY FAVORITE CRAYON COLOR

BLUE IS THE COLOR OF A BIG WHALE

BLUE IS THE COLOR OF MY
FAVORITE JEANS I LIKE TO WEAR

BLUE IS MY FAVORITE COLOR
OF BALLOONS

BLUE IS THE COLOR OF
JERRY THE JELLYFISH

Made in the USA
Las Vegas, NV
02 November 2023